THE GREATES[T JOURNEY]
ESSENTIAL COLLECTION

MW00526815

LISA * CHLOË * ALEX * MÁIRÉAD * LYNN

Arranged by Carol Tornquist

Produced by
Alfred Music Publishing Co., Inc.
P.O. Box 10003
Van Nuys, CA 91410-0003
alfred.com

Printed in USA.

ISBN-10: 0-7390-6963-2
ISBN-13: 978-0-7390-6963-9

CONTENTS

Bonus Songs

AVE MARIA

Words and Music by
J.S. Bach and Charles Gounod
Arranged by David Downes
Arranged by Carol Tornquist

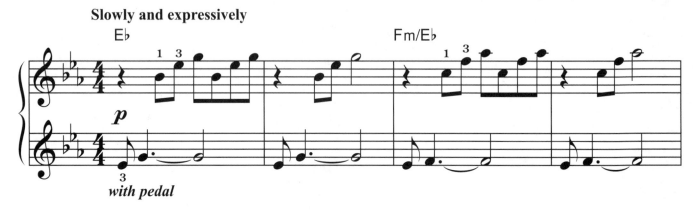

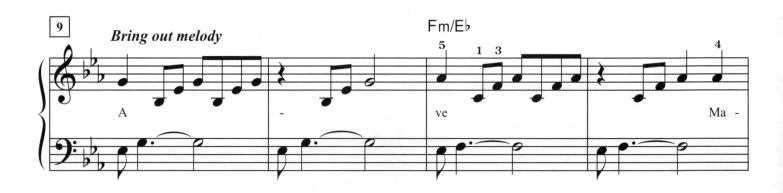

BEYOND THE SEA

Original Words and Music by
Charles Trenet and Albert Lasry
English Words by Jack Lawrence
Arranged by Carol Tornquist

Slowly, with simplicity

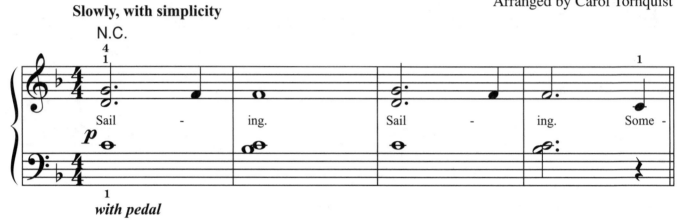

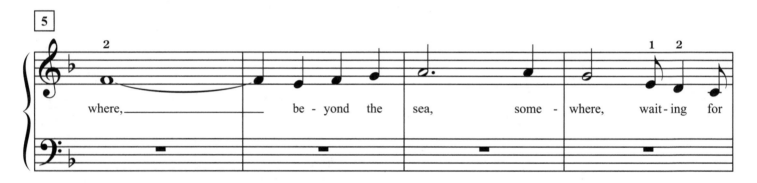

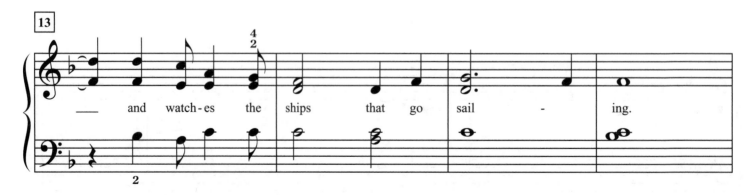

THE BUTTERFLY

Traditional
Arranged by David Downes
Arranged by Carol Tornquist

Lively and accented

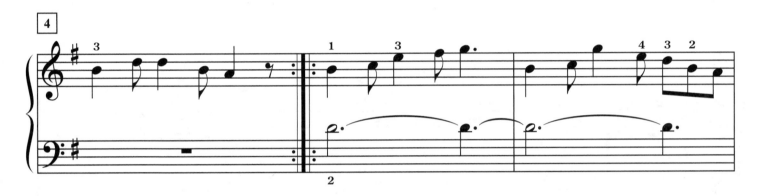

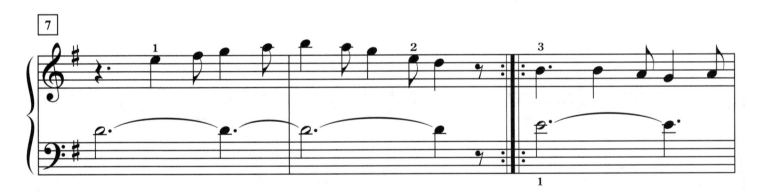

Suddenly faster, with energy

THE CALL

Words and Music by
David Downes and Brendan Graham
Arranged by Carol Tornquist

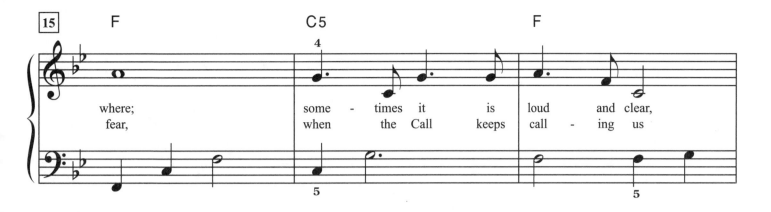

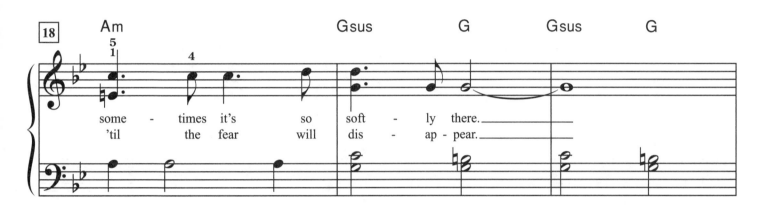

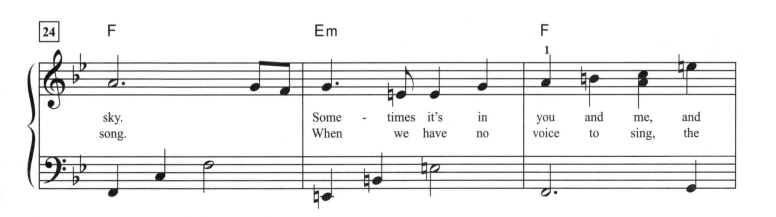

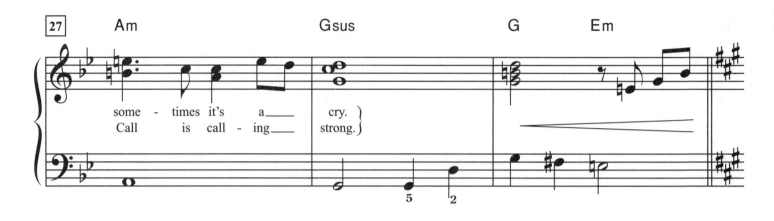

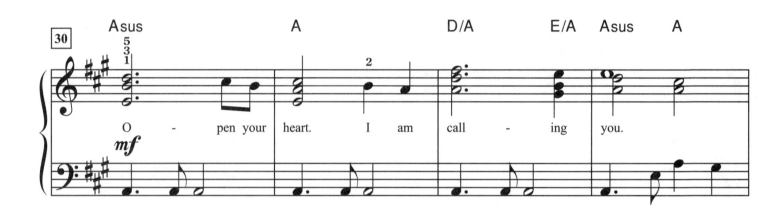

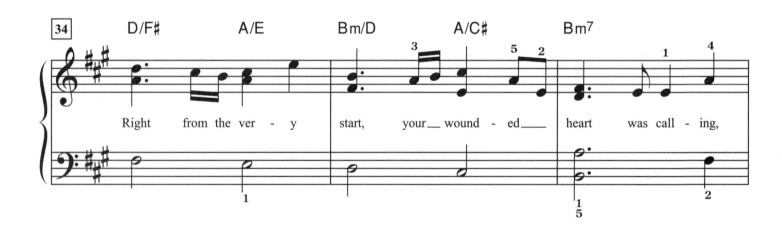

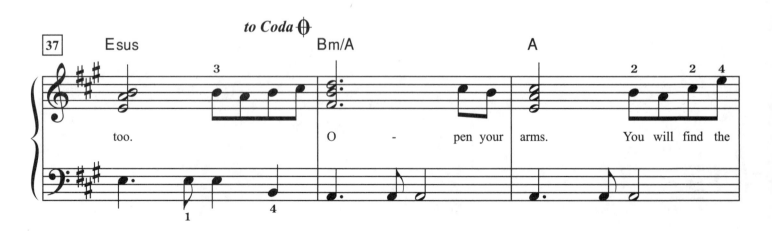

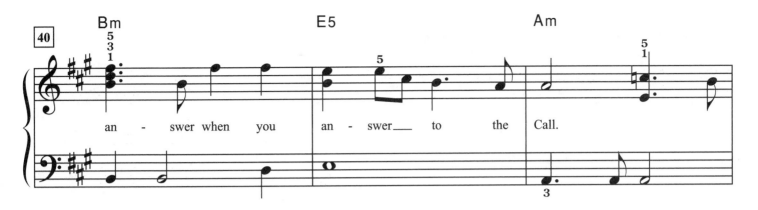

an - swer when you an - swer___ to the Call.

D.S. al Coda

Coda

O - pen your arms. You will find the an - swer when you

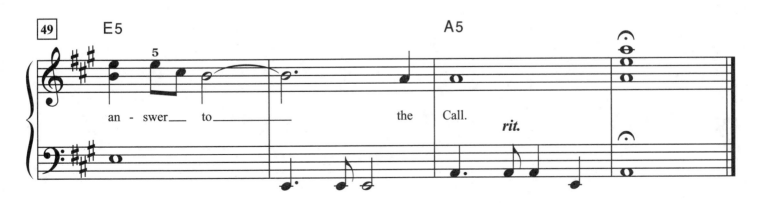

an - swer___ to_____ the Call. *rit.*

DANNY BOY

Traditional
Text by Frederick Weatherly
Arranged by Carol Tornquist

24

DÚLAMAN

Traditional
Arranged by David Downes
Arranged by Carol Tornquist

Dú - la - mán na bin - ne buí, dú - la - mán_____ Gae - lach._____

Dú - la - mán ba far - rai - ge, b'fhaerr_____ a bhí in Éir - inn. Tá

N.C.

ceann_____ buí óir ar an_____ dú - la - mán_____ gae - lach, Ta

dhá_____ chlu - ais mhaol ar an dú - la - mán_____ maor - ach.

Dú - la - mán na bin - ne buí, dú - la - mán Gae - lach.

Dú - la - mán na farr - ai - ge, b'fhearr a bhi in Éir - inn.

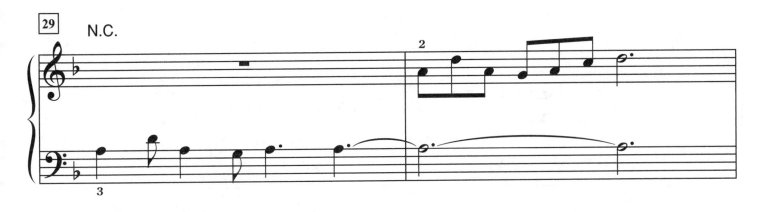

N.C.

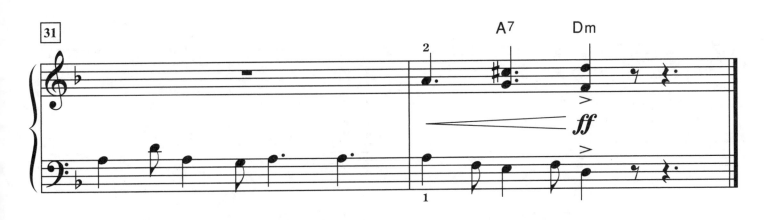

A7 Dm

GREEN THE WHOLE YEAR 'ROUND

Words and Music by
David Downes and Shay Healy
Arranged by Carol Tornquist

Slowly, with expression

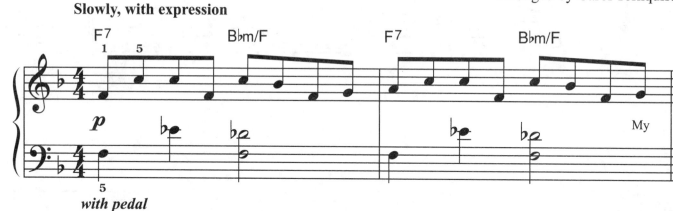

with pedal

true - love sits in a for - est glade in the spring-time's gold - en light. The

flow'rs, they dance in the gen - tle breeze and the warm sun shines so bright. And of

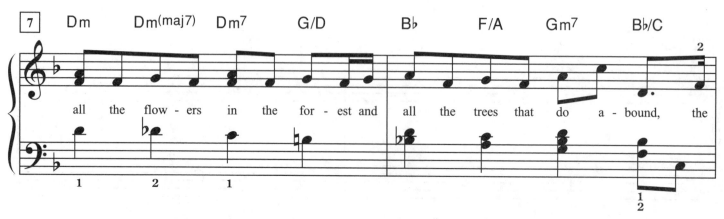

all the flow - ers in the for - est and all the trees that do a - bound, the

32

THEME FROM "HARRY'S GAME"

Words and Music by
Ciaran Brennan and Paul Brennan
Arranged by Carol Tornquist

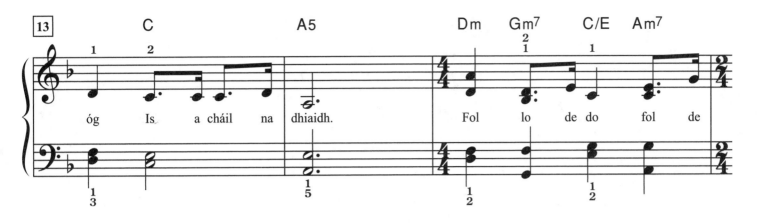

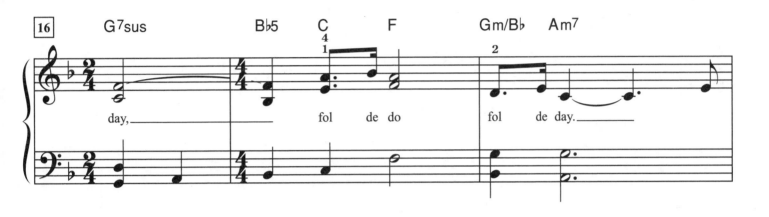

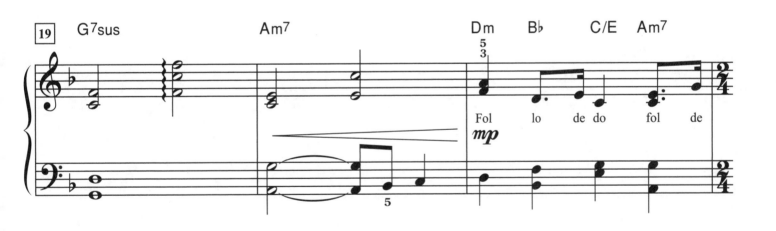

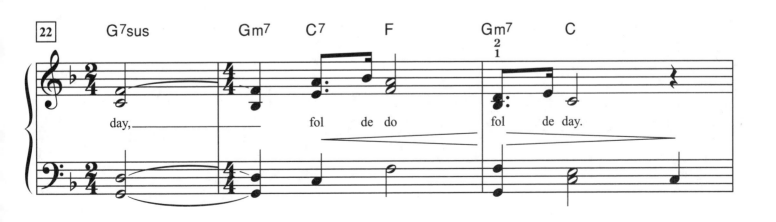

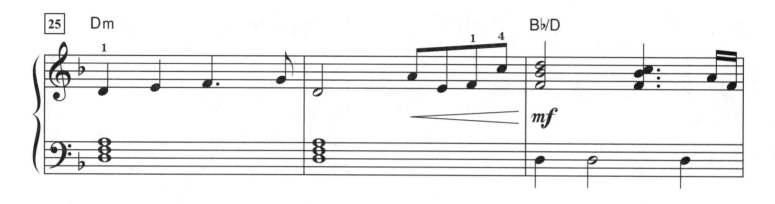

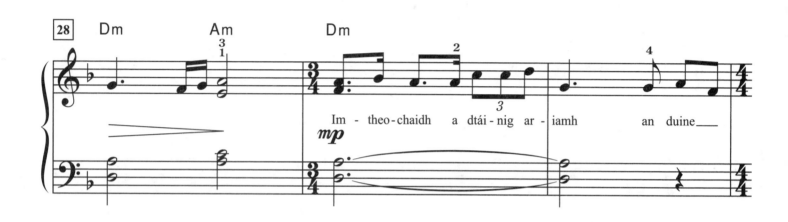

Im - theo - chaidh a dtái - nig ar - iamh an duine___

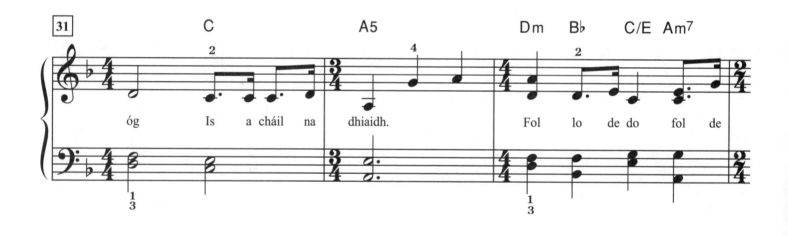

óg   Is   a cháil na   dhiaidh.   Fol   lo de do   fol de

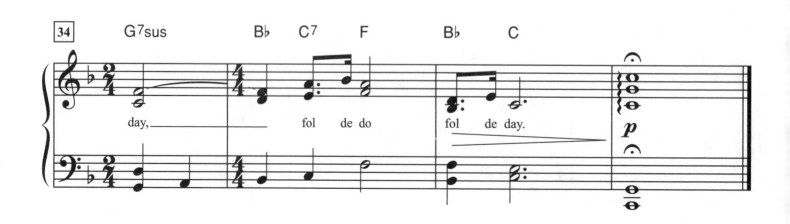

day,___   fol   de do   fol de day.

MO GHILE MEAR

Traditional
Arranged by David Downes,
Barry McCrea and Caitriona Nidhubhghaill
Arranged by Carol Tornquist

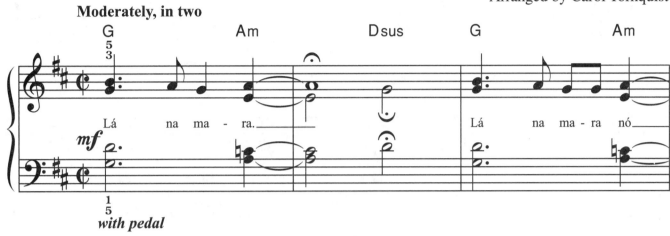

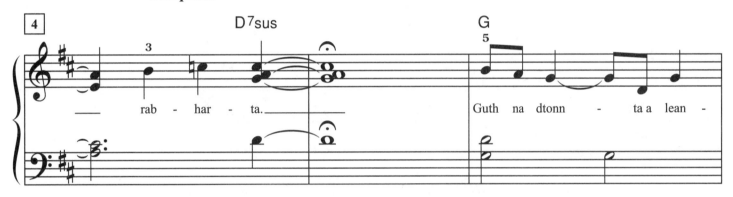

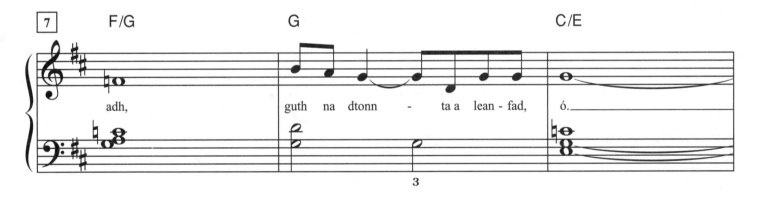

38

ISLE OF INISFREE

Words and Music by Dick Farrelly
Arranged by Carol Tornquist

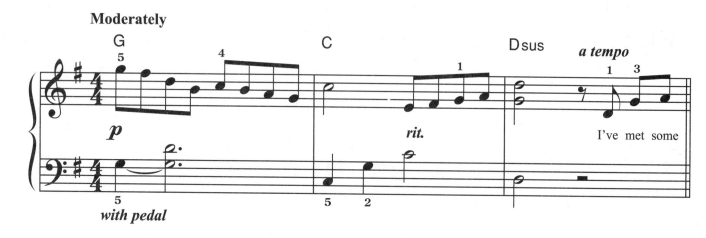

46

ORINOCO FLOW

Words and Music by
Enya, Nicky Ryan, and Roma Ryan
Arranged by Carol Tornquist

SOMEWHERE

(from *West Side Story*)

Music by Leonard Bernstein
Lyrics by Stephen Sondheim
Arranged by Carol Tornquist

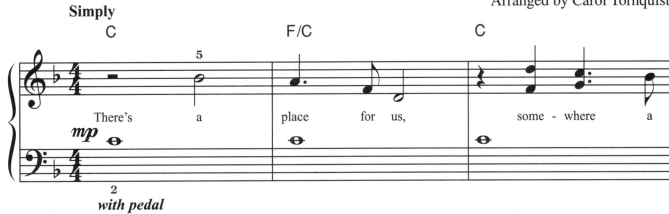

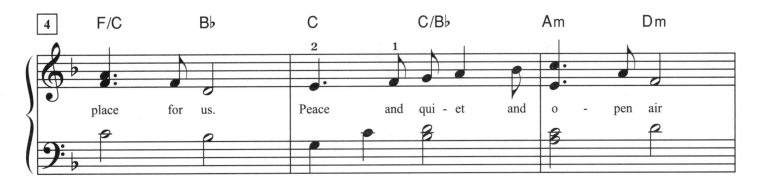

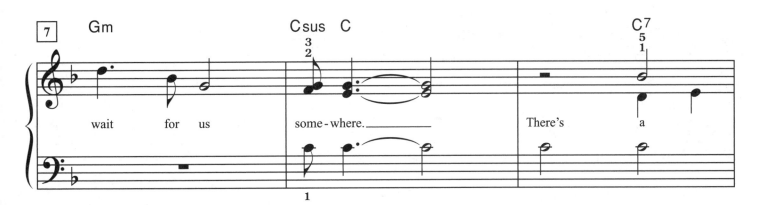

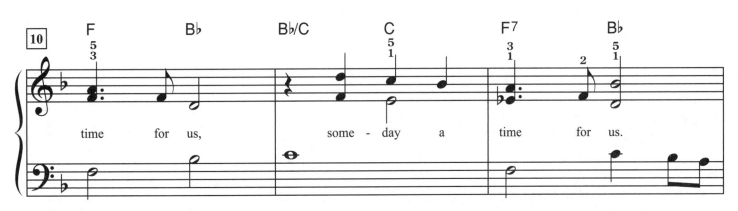

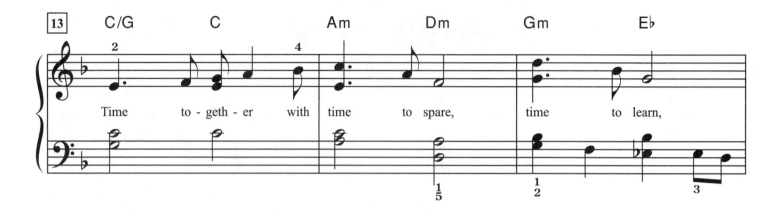

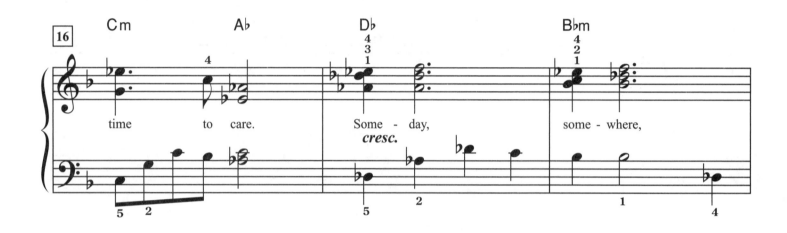

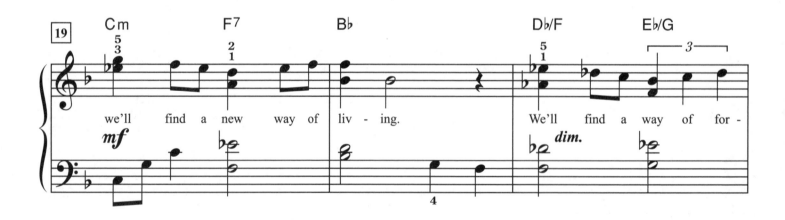

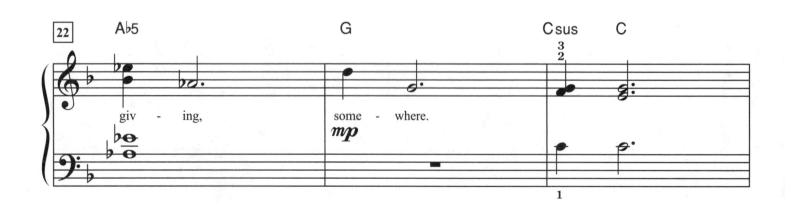

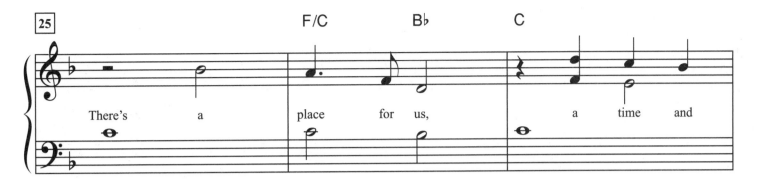

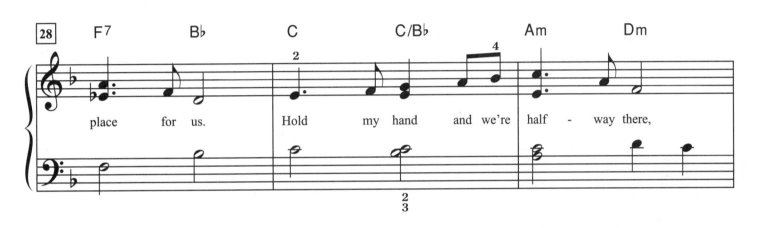

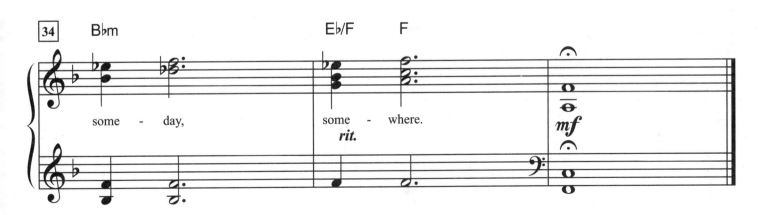

PIE JESU

(from *Requiem*)

Traditional
Arranged by Andrew Lloyd Webber
Arranged by Carol Tornquist

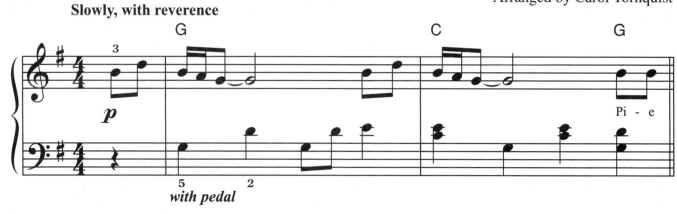

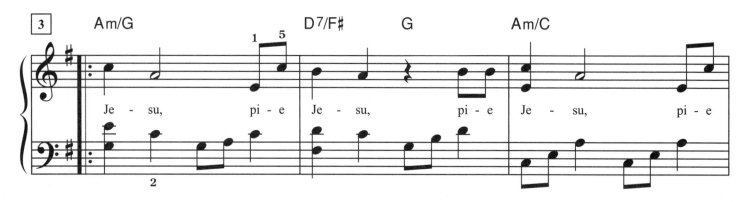

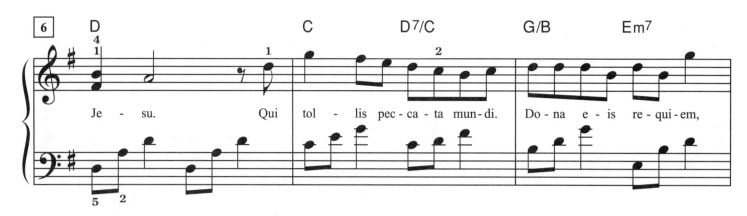

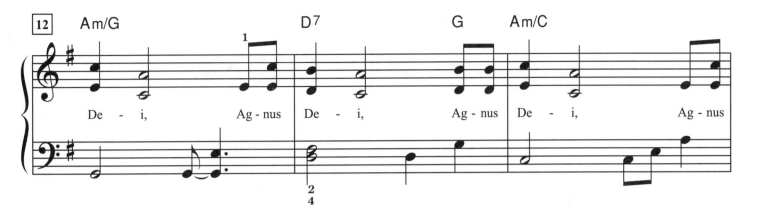

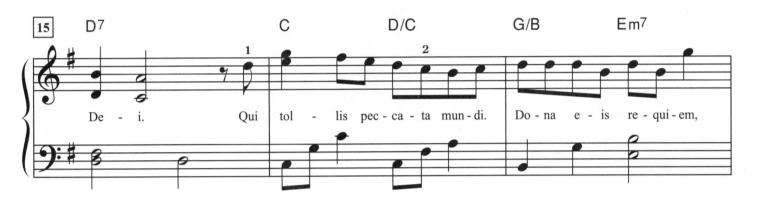

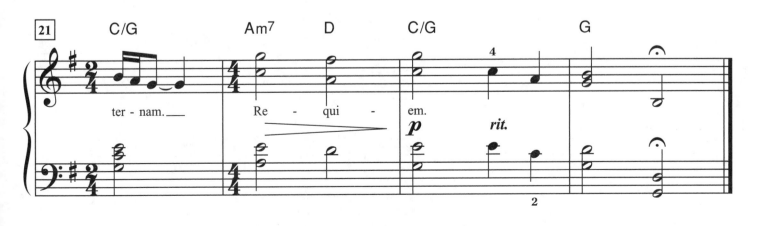

SHENANDOAH – THE CONTRADICTION

Traditional
Arranged by David Downes
and Mairead Nesbitt
Arranged by Carol Tornquist

Slowly and freely

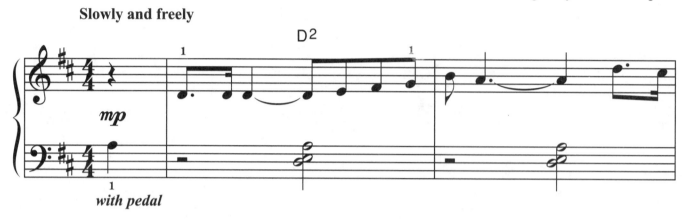

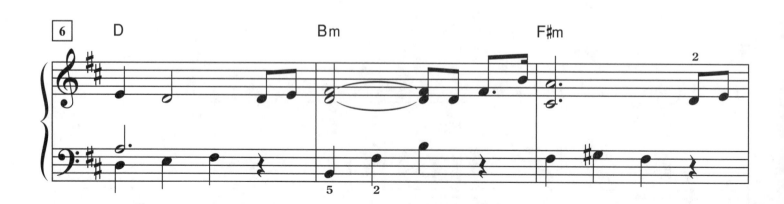

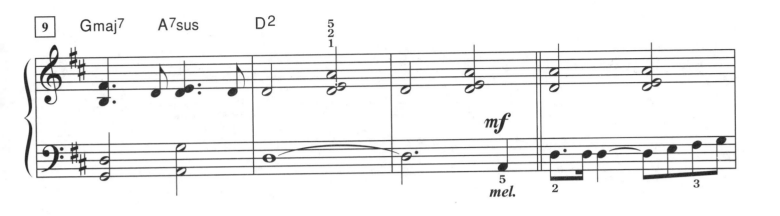

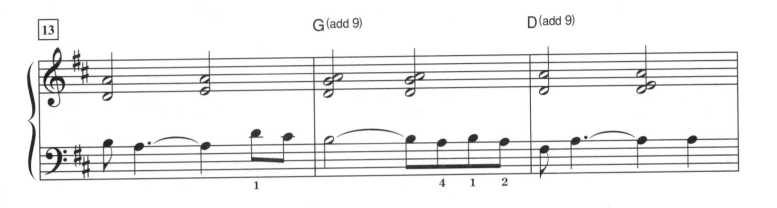

"The Contradiction"
Brightly, in two

THE SKY AND THE DAWN AND THE SUN

Words and Music by
David Downes and Brendan Graham
Arranged by Carol Tornquist

62

SPANISH LADY

Traditional
Arranged by David Downes
Arranged by Carol Tornquist

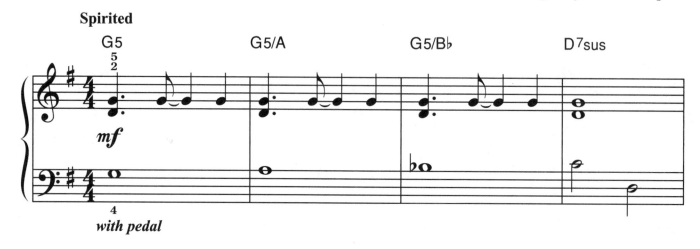

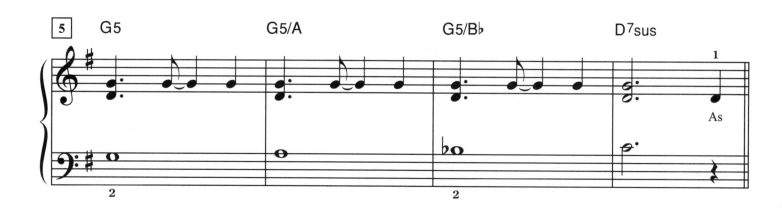

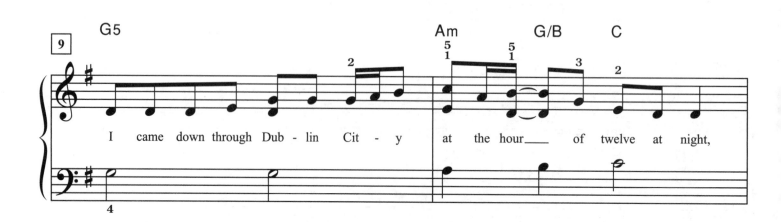

I came down through Dub-lin Cit-y at the hour___ of twelve at night,

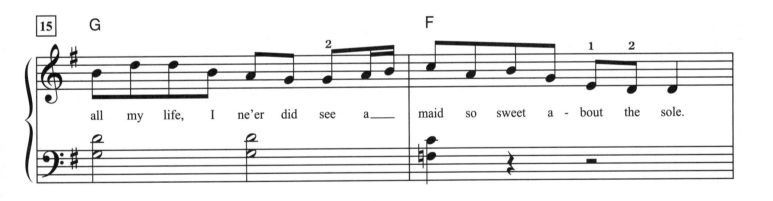

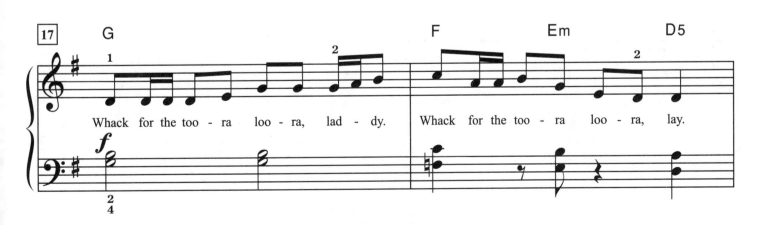

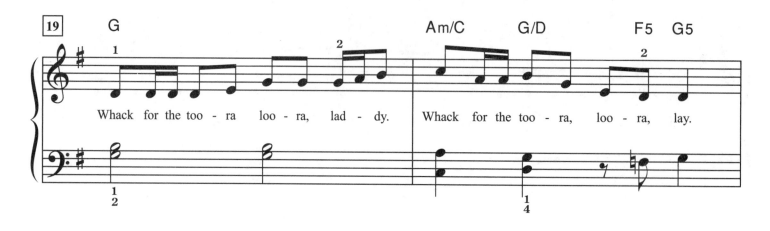

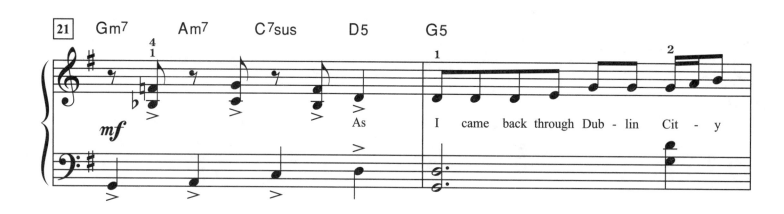

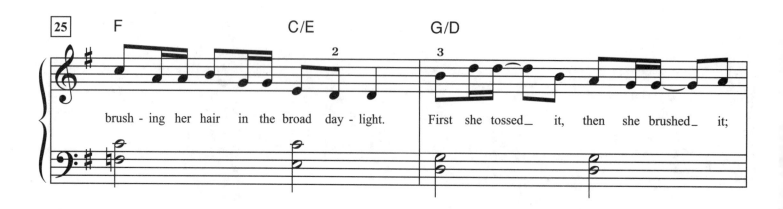

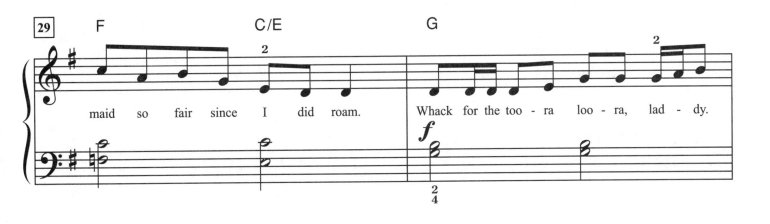

THE VOICE

Words and Music by Brendan Graham
Arranged by Carol Tornquist

72

YOU RAISE ME UP

Words and Music by
Rolf Lovland and Brendan Graham
Arranged by Carol Tornquist

Moderately slow

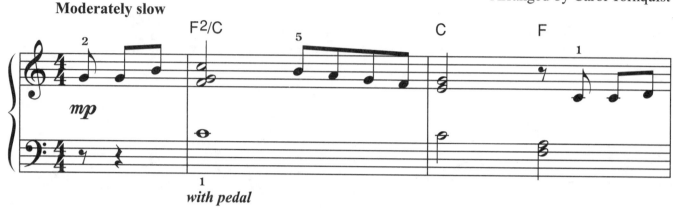

with pedal

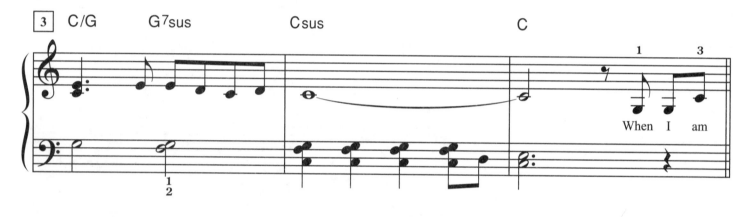

When I am

down   and, oh, my soul so   wea-ry,_____ when trou-bles come   and my heart___ bur-dened

be,_____ then I am still   and wait here___ in the si - lence   un - til you